The Missing Kitten

The Missing Kitten

Holly Webb

Illustrated by Sophy Williams

SCHOLASTIC INC.

For Emily and the gorgeous Rosie Bumble

ISBN 978-0-545-90370-7

10 9 8 7 6 5 4 3 2 1   16 17 18 19 20

Printed in the U.S.A.   40
This edition first printing 2016

Chapter One

Scarlett looked around her new bedroom with delight. It was huge! And because it was up in the roof of the cottage, it was a really interesting shape, all ups and downs. There was a gorgeous window, with a curly handle to open it, and a big, wide windowsill she could sit on. Her old bedroom had been tiny, and a kind of squarish shape.

"Nice, right?" Jackson, her big brother, put his head around the door. He had the bedroom next to hers, which was basically the other half of the roof space. Mom and Dad had said that their bedrooms used to be the attic.

"I love it," Scarlett said happily. "The window's the best thing! I love seeing all the fields and trees, and look! Cows! Outside my bedroom window!"

Jackson chuckled. "Cows not cars. Now *that's* a change! Yeah, it's great. Except everything's a little far away."

Scarlett nodded slowly. "There *is* a store in the village," she reminded him.

Jackson made a face. "Yeah, one store! And a blacksmith. How weird is that?"

"And the school's in the village, too," Scarlett added, very quietly. "I wish we didn't have to change schools." That was the thing she was least happy about with their move to the country. She was really going to miss her old school, and her friends. Lucy and Ella had said they'd come and stay during vacation, but that was a long time from now. And meanwhile, she was going to start at a school where she didn't know anyone, and she certainly didn't have any friends.

"It'll be all right," Jackson told her cheerfully, and Scarlett sighed. He wasn't worried. He never was. Jackson was really into sports, and he found it very easy to make friends. But he didn't show off, so people just wanted to hang out with him. Scarlett wished she knew how he did it.

"Did you hear that rustling noise?" Jackson pointed up at the ceiling. "I bet there are mice in all that thatch. Remember to tell Mom and Dad about that, Scarlett. You need to start working on them again about a kitten, now that we're here. They said maybe after we'd moved, didn't they?"

Scarlett grinned at him. "I know! I thought I'd maybe give them a day, though, before I started asking. Let them get some boxes unpacked first…" She looked up, too. "Do you really think there are mice?"

Jackson gazed thoughtfully at the ceiling. "Probably. It sounds like it to me. Unless it's a rat, of course."

"Uuurgh! OK, I'll ask Mom now. No way am I living in a house with a rat!" Scarlett shuddered.

"I'm with you on that," Jackson grinned. "Rats can be pretty big, you know. Bigger than a kitten, anyway." He made a ratty face, pulling his lips back to show big ratty teeth.

"Stop it!" Scarlett cried. "Maybe we can get a grown-up cat, then. I don't mind if it isn't a little kitten. I'd just love to have any kind of cat, and they did say maybe we could. You'll help, won't you? You'll ask, too?"

Jackson nodded. "Yeah. Although I don't want to come down in the morning to find a row of dead mice on the doormat. That's what Sam says his cat does."

Scarlett looked worried. "I think I'd rather have a cat that just scares the mice away…"

Scarlett started her kitten campaign while everyone was sitting down eating lunch. It felt really odd seeing their old kitchen table in a completely different kitchen.

"It's so quiet," Mom said happily, looking out of the open window. "I don't think I've heard a single car since we got here. I love it that we're down at the end of the lane."

"I keep thinking there's something missing," Dad admitted. "But it'll be great once we're used to it. And the air smells amazing."

Jackson sniffed loudly. "That's the cows, Dad."

Scarlett made a face at him. She didn't want him distracting Mom and Dad—this was a great opportunity to mention a kitten. She took a deep breath. "It's not a lot like Laurence Road, is it?" she said, thinking about their old home. "With all the busy traffic..." She swallowed, and glanced hopefully from Mom to Dad and back again. "You wouldn't worry about a cat getting run over here, would you?"

Dad snorted with laughter and turned to Mom. "You win, Laura. She lasted more than an hour."

Scarlett blinked. "What do you mean?"

Mom reached out an arm and hugged her around the shoulder. "Dad and I were talking about it last night, Scarlett. We wondered how long you'd be able to wait before you asked about a cat. I said that I thought it would be once we'd settled in a little, and Dad said you'd ask the moment we got here. So I won, and now he has to cook dinner tonight!"

"Simple. Hamburgers," Dad said.

Mom smiled at him. "You do realize

it's a twenty-minute drive to the nearest hamburger joint now, don't you?"

"You mean you were just waiting for me to ask? So can we have one?" Scarlett said hopefully, eager to get back to talking about kittens.

Mom nodded. "Yes. But we can't go to an animal shelter tomorrow—we need to do some unpacking, and besides, I don't have a clue where the nearest one is."

"I can find out!" Scarlett said eagerly. "It's just—it would be really nice to have time to get to know the kitten before school starts. We've only got two weeks, and then Jackson and I won't be at home for most of the day."

Dad nodded. "I know, Scarlett, but I don't think we'll be able to find you a kitten right now. I know it would be nice to have one while you're still at home. But it won't be a huge problem if you're at school. Mom'll be at work, but I'll be at home working, so the kitten won't be lonely. And your new school's really close. You'll be home in ten minutes."

Scarlett nodded. That was another thing that was different, being able to walk to school. Mom and Dad had even said she and Jackson could walk on their own, if they wanted, since it was all along footpaths.

"I suppose." Scarlett nodded. "So we can really have a cat? You actually mean it? We can look for one?"

"Promise," Dad told her solemnly.

Scarlett beamed at him. She could

come home from school and play with her cat. Her own cat! She'd wanted to have one for so long, and now it was going to happen.

"Scarlett! I'm off to the village," Dad yelled up the stairs.

Scarlett shoved an armful of T-shirts into a drawer, and dashed out of her room. "I'm coming!"

She really wanted to walk there. They'd seen the village a couple of times before. The first time was when they came to look at the house. Mom had gotten her new job at the hospital, and Mom and Dad explained that they would need to move, since it was too far for her to drive every day. Scarlett had really missed her for those few weeks when she'd been leaving early and not getting back until it was almost time for Scarlett to go to bed. Now that they'd moved, the hospital was only half an hour away, in the nearest big town to their tiny little village. Once they'd made the decision that Mom would take the job, and agreed to buy the cottage, Scarlett and Jackson had gone for a day's visit at their new school and seen the village again. But Scarlett had been so nervous about the school, she couldn't remember what it was like.

"It's so pretty," she murmured as they walked along the path. "Look at all the flowers. I saw a rabbit last night,

Dad, did I tell you?"

"Only about six times! I almost had a heart attack when you screamed like that. I thought you'd fallen out of the window."

"Sorry! I was excited! I've never seen a rabbit in my yard before!" Scarlett giggled. "Can we go down here? Is it the right way?"

Dad nodded. "Yup, this is the quickest path down to the village, the way you and Jackson will go to school, probably."

Scarlett swallowed nervously. She was still worrying about the school. It was tiny, which was nice, she supposed. There wouldn't be that many people to get to know. But they'd probably all been together since preschool. They might not want a stranger joining their class at all.

Dad nudged her gently with his elbow. "You had a good time on your visit, didn't you?"

Scarlett looked up at him, surprised.

"It was pretty obvious what you were thinking, sweetheart."

"I suppose. Yes. Everyone was nice. But that was just one morning. I have to go there every day…"

"It'll be great. You'll be fine, I'm sure you will."

Scarlett nodded. She didn't really want to think about it. "Look—is that the village? I can see houses." She ran on ahead. "And there's the store, Dad, look."

"I'd better find the list," Dad muttered, searching his pockets. "We definitely need bread. Can you be in charge of finding that for me? Now, where on earth did I put it?"

But Scarlett wasn't listening. She had seen something—a notice board in the store window. It was full of advertisements—exercise classes in the church hall, someone offering to make celebration cakes, an almost new lawnmower for sale…

And a litter of kittens, three black-and-white, one orange, ready to leave their mother now, free to good homes.

Chapter Two

"Dad! Look!" Scarlett was so excited, she couldn't keep still—she was dancing from foot to foot, pointing at the notice.

"What?" Her dad hurried up, peering into the window. "Oh! I can see why you're so excited. 'Ready now,' hmm?" He read the ad thoughtfully, and then got his phone out.

"Are you going to call them?" Scarlett squeaked excitedly.

"No. I'm going to put the number into my phone, get some bread and milk, and go home and talk it over with your mother. Can you imagine what she'd say if we went out shopping and came home with a kitten?"

Scarlett sighed. "I guess you're right. It would be funny, though." She giggled. "'Hi, Mom, here's the milk . . .' And we take a kitten out of the bag!"

"It could have been here a while, this notice," Dad pointed out. "The kittens might all have gone. Don't get your hopes up, OK?"

Scarlett nodded. But as they paid for the shopping, she took a deep breath and smiled at the lady behind the counter. She hated talking to people she didn't know, but this was important. "Excuse me, but you see the notice in the window about the kittens? Has it been up for long—I mean, do you know if they still have any left?"

The lady beamed at her. "Looking for a kitten, are you? Julie Mallins will be pleased. She only put the notice up earlier this week, and I know she's still looking for homes for them all."

"Really?" Scarlett was dancing around again—she just couldn't help it. "Oh, Dad, can we go home and talk to Mom about it now, please?"

"All right, all right!" Dad grinned, raising his eyebrows at the lady.

Scarlett ran all the way home—in fact, she went twice as far as Dad did, because he wouldn't run, too, so she kept having to turn around and run all the way back to him to tell him to hurry up. When she raced in through the front of the cottage, she was completely out of breath.

"Mom! Mom!" she gasped, running from the living room to the kitchen and back to the bottom of the stairs.

"What's the matter, sweetheart?" Her mom backed out of the understairs closet, where she'd been putting coats and boots away. "Scarlett, you're scarlet!" It was an old family joke.

"Ha-ha. Mom, there's someone in the village who has a litter of kittens she wants to give away!"

"Really?"

"There was a flyer up in the village store." Dad came in, holding out his phone. "I've got the number—what do you think?"

Scarlett bit her lip to stop herself shrieking, "Please, please, please." Her mom was very firm about not whining, and she really didn't want to get on the wrong side of her right now.

"Well, I suppose we could ask to go and look at them..." her mom said, rather doubtfully. "I'm just a little worried that the house is all upside down right now while we're still unpacking. Wouldn't that be stressful for a kitten?"

Scarlett's face fell. Mom was right. "Maybe we could wait?" she whispered. "Maybe we could just choose a kitten and ask them to keep it for us a little longer?" She really wanted to have a kitten now, but she didn't want their new pet to start out scared by all the boxes everywhere.

Dad hugged her. "Well, let's see what Julie says—she's the owner," he explained to Mom. "She might not think it's a problem. To be honest, we've done most of the unpacking in the kitchen already. We could keep it in there for the time being—I think you have to keep new kittens in one room to start off with anyway."

Mom nodded. "I forgot about that. We used to have a cat when I was little," she told Scarlett, "but it was such a long time ago. We'll all have to learn how to look after a cat together."

"What?" Jackson put his head around the kitchen door. "Are we getting one? What's happening?"

"Scarlett found a flyer about a litter of kittens needing homes," Dad told him. "We should have known—if there were kittens around, Scarlett was bound to find them! Should I call this woman then?"

Mom nodded, and Scarlett flung her arms around her. She held her breath and listened as Dad made the phone call.

"Hi, is this Julie? We saw your sign about the kittens…Mmm…We wondered if we'd be able to come and see them? Uh-huh. Well, now's great, if that's really OK with you. Fantastic. Kendall's Lane. Oh, off the main road? See you in about ten minutes, then."

Scarlett gasped. Ten minutes! Ten minutes till they saw their kitten!

"Here they are."

Julie turned out to be a really sweet lady who'd adopted Goldie, the kittens' mom, after finding her eating scraps of bread under her birdbath, because she was a stray and so hungry.

"It took weeks to even get her to

come inside," Julie told Scarlett as she led them through to the kitchen. "But she's settling down now. I think she knew she needed to let someone look after her, so she could have her kittens somewhere nice and warm."

"How old are the kittens?" Scarlett's mom asked as Julie opened the kitchen door.

"Ten weeks—the vet said they should be fine to go to new homes," Scarlett heard Julie say. But she wasn't really concentrating. Instead, she was staring at the basket in the corner, where a beautiful brownish cat was curled up with four kittens mounded around and on top of her.

"Goodness, she looks tired," Mom murmured.

"Yes, I think she is, poor thing. She's been a really good mom, but she was so thin to start with, apart from her huge tummy full of kittens. I was worried that she wouldn't be able to feed them, but she's done very well. They're all practically weaned now—they love their food!"

Woken by the voices, one of the kittens popped his head up, his big orange ears twitching with interest.

"Oh, just look at him!" Scarlett whispered. "His ears are too big for him!"

Julie nodded. "I know, he's cute, isn't he? He's got huge paws, too; I think he's going to be a really big cat."

The kitten gently nudged the brother or sister next to him with the side of his chin, and the rest of the kittens popped up in a line, staring at Scarlett and Jackson.

The other three were black and white, very pretty, without the big ears. They had enormous whiskers instead—great big white mustaches of them.

"I like the orange one," Jackson said. "That one's a boy, right?"

Julie nodded. "Yes, and the three black-and-white ones are all girls."

"I like him, too," Scarlett agreed. "Will they let us pet them? Is that OK?"

"They're usually very friendly. Especially Ginger."

"Oh, is that what he's called?" Scarlett

tried not to sound disappointed. She would have liked to choose a name together for their kitten—Ginger was what a lot of orange cats were called!

"Oh, no. I've tried not to give them names—I'm hoping to find homes for them all, and if I name them I'll just want to keep them. But it's hard not to think of him as Ginger."

The orange kitten was standing up now, arching his back and stretching as he climbed out of the basket. He looked sideways at Scarlett with his big blue eyes, to check that she was admiring how handsome he was as he stretched. She was watching him eagerly, and she gave a little sigh of delight as he stepped toward her, gently rubbing himself against her arm.

"Oh, he's got boots!" Scarlett looked over at Jackson and her mom and dad. "Look, he has furry white boots on!"

Mom laughed. "It does look like that," she agreed. "Those are very cute."

"I know lots of cats have white paws, but I've never seen one where the white goes that far up before." Scarlett stroked the kitten lovingly, and his black-and-white sisters followed him out of the basket, looking for some attention, too. Their mother stared watchfully after them, then seemed to decide that Scarlett and the others weren't dangerous to her babies. She gave a huge yawn and curled up for a nap.

The girl kittens let Scarlett's mom and dad pet them, then they set off chasing after a feathery cat toy, racing around the kitchen and batting it ahead of them with their paws. The orange kitten watched them, but he didn't join in. Instead, he placed a hopeful paw on Scarlett's knee, and she looked back at him, just as hopefully. Did he want to be picked up?

"He's very cuddly," Julie said quietly. "He's a real people cat. Try to put him on your lap."

Scarlett gently wrapped her hands around his middle. Even though he was the biggest of the kittens, he still felt tiny—so light, as though there was nothing to him.

The kitten gave a pleased little squeak and padded his fat white paws up and down her jeans as though he was testing how comfy she was. Scarlett found herself smoothing her jeans, wanting him to think she was nice to sit on. He padded all the way around in a circle a couple of times, and then wobbled and flopped down, stretching his front paws out and flexing his claws gently in and out of the denim fabric of her jeans.

"That tickles!" Scarlett giggled, petting him under his little white chin.

The kitten purred delightedly. That was the best place, the spot where he was always itchy. He pointed his chin to the ceiling and purred louder, telling her to keep going.

Jackson joined in, running one finger gently down the kitten's back. "His fur's really soft. And look at his paws! They're bright pink underneath!" The kitten was enjoying the attention so much that he'd collapsed into a happy heap on his side, purring like a steam train.

Scarlett looked down at his paws and laughed—they really were pink. A sort of pinkish-apricot color, and so soft and smooth looking.

"They'll probably get a bit darker once he starts going outside," Julie explained. "They've only been indoors so far. He'd need to stay in for a bit longer if you decide to take him." She looked at Scarlett's mom and dad.

Scarlett and Jackson got up, then both turned to look at them, too, and their mom laughed. She turned to Julie and asked hopefully, "I don't suppose you could lend us some cat litter, could you? The store in the village would have cat food…"

"You mean we can take him now?" Scarlett gasped.

Her mom shrugged. "Why not?"

Chapter Three

"Dad, we're almost out of Bootle's food. There's only the salmon flavor left, and I don't think he liked that one very much."

Bootle wrapped himself lovingly around Scarlett's legs. He knew just what was in those cans, and he didn't see any reason why he shouldn't have a second breakfast.

Calling him Bootle had been Jackson's idea. Scarlett had suggested Boots, but it was like Ginger—a little bit too everyday for such a special cat. Bootle was much better.

Jackson looked up from his huge pile of toast. "We could go to the store," he said. "I've almost finished the bread, and there's not a lot for lunch."

"I've got a work call in a few minutes," said Dad. He looked at them thoughtfully. "Though I suppose you guys could go if you like."

"On our own?" Scarlett stared at him.

"Why not? You were going to try it when school started next week, weren't you? If you're careful, and you stick together."

Scarlett shut her eyes for a second at

the mention of school. She was trying not to think about it. "Will you look after Bootle while we're out?" she said seriously.

"Scarlett! You'll only be gone half an hour!" Dad grinned.

"But he's not used to me not being here!" It was true. Scarlett had spent all of her time with Bootle since they'd brought him home, only leaving him at nighttime, when he was safely tucked in his cardboard box. It was padded with an old towel and a hot water bottle to feel like his mother and the other kittens. Just until he got used to them not being next to him.

"I think it would be good for him to see you go out," her dad said gently. "I know you don't want to think about school, Scarlett, but you do go on Monday. Bootle's had a whole week of you around all the time. He needs to learn to be without you."

"But he'll be lonely," Scarlett said worriedly.

"It's only for half an hour," Dad reminded her.

"When we're back at school it won't be!"

"Then he'll have me for company while I'm working. And you know how he loves the computer."

Scarlett smiled. It was true. Bootle was fascinated by Dad's computer. He seemed to love the way the keys went up and down. He would sit watching Dad type forever, just occasionally putting out a paw to try to join in. Then he would look miffed when Dad told him no. Secretly, Scarlett was planning to let him try one day when she was using the laptop she shared with Jackson. She wanted to see what Bootle would write—she knew it would probably be a string of random letters, but she was hoping for a secret message!

"Come on." Jackson stuffed the last of the toast into his mouth. "Can we get some chips while we're at the store, Dad?"

"Mmm-hmm. Here." Dad gave Jackson some money. "But I do want change. Be back by ten-thirty, all right? I don't want to be pacing up and down outside looking for you."

"Are you really worried about school?" Jackson asked Scarlett as they wandered down the footpath in the direction of the village.

"A little." Scarlett sighed. "What if nobody talks to me?"

"Why wouldn't they?" Jackson asked, shrugging.

Scarlett shook her head. He was trying to be nice, but he just didn't get it.

"You had lots of friends at your old school," said Jackson. "Why do you think you won't make friends here?"

"It's such a little school," Scarlett tried to explain. "Only one class in each year, and not that many in each class, either. They'll all know each other so well. Like I know Lucy and Ella." She wished she was as confident as Jackson. He'd already managed to go out for a walk and found a couple of boys playing soccer. He'd joined in, and then he'd gone back to their house. Scarlett wasn't sure how he did it.

Jackson rolled his eyes. "Come on. We're almost there."

They went into the store, and Jackson went to look at soccer magazines, while Scarlett found the cat food. Then she realized that there were a couple of other girls standing behind her.

"Who's she?" one of them whispered.

"Don't you remember? It's that new girl. The one who came to school for a morning."

"Ohhh! What's she called?"

"It was something weird. Amber or something."

Scarlett felt like her stomach was squeezing into a tiny little knot inside her. That was her they were talking about. The one with the weird name. She wanted to scream, "Scarlett!" But she didn't. She grabbed a couple of cans of cat food and scuttled over to where Jackson was.

School was going to be a disaster. It was so obvious.

Scarlett lay in bed, watching her clock creep closer to seven. She'd been awake forever, worrying about their first day at school, and now she just wished it would hurry up and be time.

A throaty purr distracted her, and a soft paw patted her chin. Bootle liked her to be paying attention to him, not the clock.

"I'm glad I went downstairs and got you before breakfast," Scarlett said, tickling him behind the ears. "I know I look miserable, but you're making me feel a lot better."

Bootle closed his eyes happily and purred even louder. Scarlett knew all the places he liked to be petted, and how he particularly liked being on her bed. It was much cozier than his basket.

"I'm really going to miss you today," Scarlett murmured. "I hope you'll be OK. Dad'll look after you." She sighed a huge sigh that lifted up the quilt around her middle, and Bootle's ears twitched excitedly. He wriggled forward and peered down under the quilt. It was like a dark little nest, and he wriggled into it, just his tail sticking out and flicking from side to side.

"What are you doing?" Scarlett giggled. "Silly cat! Oh, Bootle, you're tickling my legs!"

Even the tail had disappeared now. Bootle was a plump little mound traveling around under the quilt. Then he popped out at the other end of the bed, his orange fur looking all spiky and ruffled up. He shook himself and ran a paw over his ears.

Scarlett twitched her toes under the quilt, and he stopped washing and pounced on them excitedly, jumping from side to side as she wriggled them about.

"You're awake!" Mom put her head around the door. "Time to get up, Scarlett. Hello, Bootle." She came in and patted him. "Are you worried he'll miss you while you're at school?"

Scarlett nodded, and Mom hugged her. "It'll be fine, sweetheart. Now that he's allowed in the yard he'll probably just go out and try to chase butterflies again." She looked at Scarlett. "And you'll be fine, too. Honestly. Try not to worry about it."

Scarlett nodded. But she wished she felt as sure as everybody else seemed to.

Bootle sat on the back doorstep, next to his cat flap, staring around the yard. He was confused and a little bored. Scarlett had gone somewhere. He'd known that she was going—she had picked him up and made a huge

fuss over him before she went, and
her voice had been different, as
though something was wrong.
But he hadn't expected her to
be gone this long.

He stalked around the yard,
sniffing at the grass, looking for
something interesting to do. He
sharpened his claws on the trunk
of the apple tree and tried
to climb it, but he
wasn't all that good at
climbing yet, and he only
got halfway up before he got
worried and jumped down
again. Then he had to sit and
wash for a while, pretending
to himself that he'd never meant
to climb it in the first place.

Where was she? Jackson had left, too—he preferred to play with Scarlett, but Jackson was very good at inventing games with sticks, and pieces of string to jump at.

Why had they gone away and left him? And when were they coming back?

Chapter Four

"Bootle! Did you miss me?" Scarlett picked him up and hugged him lovingly, and Bootle rubbed his head against her cheek.

Dad had come to meet them at school, since it was the first day, but tomorrow they were going to walk there and back by themselves.

"Come and have a cookie," Dad

suggested. "Then you can both tell me what it was like, now that there's no one else around." When he'd asked Scarlett at the school gate how her day was, she'd just muttered, "Fine," but he could tell she was only being polite.

"It was all right." Jackson shrugged, munching a chocolate cookie. "Played soccer at lunch. The teacher was a little strict. Shouted at people for talking. But it was fine."

Dad looked over at Scarlett, who sighed. "It was OK. This girl named Izzy was told to look after me, and she was nice. She took me around with her at break and lunchtime. But—well, it was only because she had to."

"She might really like you!" Dad pointed out.

Scarlett ran one of Bootle's huge ears between her fingers and sighed. "Maybe... It wasn't as bad as it could have been," she admitted. The two girls she'd seen in the store hadn't said anything else about her weird name, which was what she'd been worrying about. They'd been at the same table as her and Izzy at lunch, and they'd been really friendly, and asked her where she lived, and if she'd had to catch the bus to school. It turned out that lots of the children did—they came from several different villages, and a school bus went around and picked them all up.

"It's nice we can walk to school," she said to Dad, who was still looking worried about her.

Bootle rubbed himself against her red sweater, leaving orange hairs all over it, and Scarlett petted him again. Whatever happened at school, at least she could come home and play with him. She couldn't imagine being without him now.

"You're sure you wouldn't like me to come with you?" Dad asked for about the fourth time.

"No!" Jackson said. "Honestly, Dad. We're fine. It takes about ten minutes to get to school, and we don't even have to cross a road. Stop worrying."

Bootle was sitting on the bottom step of the stairs, watching disapprovingly as Scarlett and Jackson got ready. They were going again, just like yesterday! Why was he being left behind? He let out a tiny, furious mew, but Scarlett only kissed the top of his head and went out the door, leaving him with Dad.

Dad picked Bootle up and tickled his ears before rubbing the top of his head. But then he put him back down on the stairs and headed into the room where his computer was. He was going to be too busy to play again.

Bootle stalked into the kitchen and inspected his food bowl, which was empty. He had a little water, and he looked at his basket. He didn't really feel like sleeping. And if this was anything like yesterday, Scarlett and Jackson would be gone for hours.

He didn't see why he couldn't go with them. Until yesterday, he'd been with Scarlett almost all the time.

Bootle walked over to the cat flap and sniffed at it carefully. They hadn't been gone long. Maybe, if he was quick, he could follow them. Bootle shot out of the cat flap and dashed into the backyard. Scarlett and Jackson had gone out the front door, so he hurried around the side of the house and onto the little patch of front yard. He nosed his way under the blue gate, flattening himself down underneath the wooden panels and coming out into the lane, next to the car. His whiskers twitched excitedly as he tried to figure out which way Scarlett had gone. He could follow her scent, he was sure. He sniffed busily at the grass and set off running.

Scarlett and Jackson were halfway to school, walking down the path along the side of the big field, which was planted with green wheat—Scarlett hadn't known what it was, but Dad had told her.

"Did you hear a meow?" Scarlett asked suddenly, and Jackson turned around to stare at her.

"Don't be silly. Come on!"

"No, I can. I really can. It's Bootle, I'm sure." Scarlett peered along the track behind them and laughed. "It is! Look!"

Bootle was running after them, mewing happily, and as Scarlett crouched down to say hello, he clambered up into her lap and sat there, purring wearily.

He'd had to run faster than he'd ever done before to catch up.

"What's he doing here?" Jackson shook his head. "Yes, you're really smart, Bootle," he admitted, running one hand down the little orange kitten's back. "But now we have to take you back home, and we're going to be late."

"Oh, do we have to take him back?" Scarlett said sadly.

Jackson rolled his eyes. "Yes, of course we do! We can't take a cat to school, Scarlett!"

"I guess not."

"And we have to run, because we're going to be late."

Scarlett swallowed anxiously. She didn't want to be late, to have to go in after everyone else and explain what had happened. They hurried back down the path and across the lane before bursting through the front door.

Dad came out of his office, looking worried. "What's happened? Why are you back? I knew I should have gone with you!"

"Don't worry, Dad. It's fine." Scarlett held out her arms, full of purring orange kitten. "Bootle just followed us. He caught up with us as we were going past the big field—the one with wheat in it. We had to bring him back." She put Bootle into Dad's arms, and the kitten stopped purring and glared at her. He'd gone to find her, and brought her back, and now she was going again!

"Sorry, Bootle. I'd much rather stay with you." Scarlett petted his head as she went to leave.

"Come on, Scarlett," Jackson yelled from the door.

"You'd better run, sweetheart," Dad said. "I'd drive you, but by the time we've gone all around by the road, it's longer than the short cut. I'll call the school and explain why you'll be a little late. Don't worry."

"Thanks, Dad," said Scarlett.

When Scarlett and Jackson hurried into the playground, the principal, Miss Wilson, was standing at the main door watching out for them.

Scarlett was worried. Luckily, Miss Wilson didn't look upset. She just smiled at them as they raced toward her, and she patted Jackson's shoulder. "Don't worry. I used to have a dog that followed me to school. Still, I've never heard of a cat doing it. He must be very fond of you."

Scarlett nodded proudly. She hadn't really thought of it like that.

"I've explained to your teachers, so just slip quietly into your classes, all right?"

"Thanks, Miss Wilson." Scarlett crept, mouselike, along the corridor. It was all very well to say to slip in quietly, but everyone was still going to turn and stare at her. She eased open the door of her classroom, wincing as it creaked.

But her teacher, Mrs. Mason, just smiled at her, and waved her over to her table, and went on pointing out something on the whiteboard.

"I wondered where you were!" Izzy whispered to her. "I thought you might not be coming back!"

"It wasn't that bad yesterday," Scarlett muttered.

"Are you OK?" said Izzy. "Did you oversleep?"

Scarlett shook her head. "No. It sounds really stupid, but I had to take my kitten home. He followed us to school."

"Your kitten did?" Izzy stared at her. "Oh, I didn't know you had a kitten! I've got a cat. He's called Olly. But he's never followed me anywhere! He's way too lazy. What's your kitten called?"

"Bootle." Scarlett smiled proudly. "We've only had him two weeks, and he isn't used to us leaving him. Mrs. Mason's giving us a look. I'll tell you more at break, OK?"

Izzy grinned. "You're so lucky to have a kitten."

Scarlett nodded and stared at the whiteboard. Izzy was right, she realized. She really was lucky.

Chapter Five

"I'll keep Bootle inside until after you've left," Dad said at breakfast the following morning. "If I don't open the cat flap for an hour or so, and I pay him lots of attention, I'm sure he'll stay put."

"I hope so," said Mom anxiously. "We don't want him to wander too far. If he starts going out in the lane and along the paths, he could easily get lost." She glanced up at the clock. "I'd better get going. Have a lovely day, all of you. Scarlett, do you want to invite that nice girl from your class after school one day? What was she called? Izzy? I can call her mom. She could come tomorrow, maybe."

Dad nodded. "I can pick you all up from school."

Scarlett smiled. Dad had been so pleased when she'd come home the day before and said she'd actually had a good day at school. She would really like Izzy to come over.

"I'll ask her," she agreed, tickling Bootle behind the ears. He was sitting on her lap, hoping for bits of toast. He particularly liked toast with jelly, so Scarlett made sure she always had some on at least one piece now. She tore off a little corner and passed it down to him, watching him crunch it up and lick at his whiskers for crumbs.

"Do you really think Bootle will be all right?" she asked Dad anxiously. "I don't want him to be lonely."

A cautious paw reached up onto the table, aiming for more toast, and Dad snorted. "He'll be fine. He knows how to look after himself just fine. Don't you?" he added, scratching Bootle under his little white chin. "Yes, you're very sweet. Even if you are trying to steal yourself a second breakfast."

Bootle drooped his whiskers and stared at Dad, his blue eyes round and solemn.

Scarlett giggled. Bootle made it look as though he was starving to death and even Dad was almost convinced. He glanced down at his own plate of toast and then shook his head firmly.

"That kitten is a shameless liar," he told Scarlett.

Bootle prowled up and down the hallway, his tail twitching. Scarlett had left him behind again, and now his cat flap was closed. He didn't understand what was happening. Why did she have to keep going away?

"Hey! Bootle! Cat treats!" Scarlett's dad came out of the kitchen with a foil packet, and Bootle turned around hopefully. He loved those treats, especially the fishy-flavored ones. "Good boy. Yes, Scarlett said some of these might cheer you up."

Bootle laid his ears back as he heard Scarlett's name and stopped licking the treats out of Dad's hand. Scarlett! Was she about to come back? He looked at Dad hopefully.

"Oh, dear. You really do miss her, don't you?" Dad eyed him worriedly. "She'll be back later, Bootle, I promise. Come on, yummy fish things."

Bootle ate the rest of the treats, but rather slowly. He liked them, but he would have liked them much more if Scarlett had fed them to him. She had a game where she held them in front of his nose, one at a time, and he stretched up to reach. They didn't taste the same out of Dad's hand.

"Good boy, Bootle." Dad picked him up gently, took him into the office, and put him down on an old armchair. "Why don't you take a nap?"

Bootle walked around and around the seat of the chair, stamping his paws into the cushions, till eventually he slumped down and stared gloomily at the door. He didn't feel like sleeping, but he couldn't think of anything else to do.

Bootle sat in front of
the cat flap,
staring at it
hopefully and
uttering plaintive
little mews. It was
still locked. He knew
because he'd tried it, over
and over, scrabbling at the door
with his claws. But it just wouldn't open.

"Do you need to go out?" Dad asked,
coming into the kitchen and looking at
him, concerned. He crouched down next
to Bootle, who gave his knee a hopeful
nudge. "I suppose it can't hurt; it's over
an hour since Jackson and Scarlett left
for school." Dad turned the catch on the
cat flap and pushed it, showing Bootle
that it was open. "Off you go."

Bootle mewed gratefully and wriggled through the cat flap, trotting purposefully out into the backyard and straight around to the front of the house, just as he'd done the day before. Next, he was squeezing under the gate and out into the lane. This time he didn't run as fast. He knew that he'd been shut in the house a long time, and he wouldn't be able to chase Scarlett the way he had the day before.

So he padded down the path, sniffing thoughtfully here and there. It was difficult to follow the traces of Scarlett and Jackson—the cottage smelled like them, too, much more than the path, which made it confusing. But he was pretty sure they'd gone this way. Bootle bounded happily along, hoping that they would be in the field again, perhaps sitting down, waiting for him.

But no one was there. Bootle walked up and down the edge of the huge field, staring anxiously into the green stalks. Was Scarlett in there? She might be, but he couldn't smell her, or hear her. He slipped in between two rows of wheat, pushing his way through the green stalks and mewing.

Then his ears twitched. There was a scuffling noise ahead of him, and a small bird fluttered out of the wheat, making Bootle leap back in surprise. He'd seen birds in the yard, but never up close. He hissed at it, but the bird was already half hopping, half flying away. Bootle followed it sadly out of the wheat stalks. He didn't think Scarlett was here.

Glancing around the narrow path at the edge of the field, he tried to remember what Scarlett had been doing when he ran after her yesterday. They had been walking along here, away from him, as though they were making for the hedge at the end of the field.

Determinedly, Bootle padded along, hopping over the ruts and big clumps of grass and keeping a hopeful eye out for Scarlett. At the corner of the field there was a gap in the hedge, and then a short muddy lane leading out onto a paved road. Bootle had never really seen a road, and he jumped back, his whiskers bristling, as a car roared past. He had been in a car when he left his mom to come to Scarlett's house, and then when he'd had to go to the vet for his vaccinations, but both times he had been in a basket. From kitten height, the cars going along the road were enormous, and terrifyingly noisy.

He crept into the muddy lane, eyeing the opening out onto the pavement. His ears were laid nervously back, but at the same time Bootle breathed out the faintest little purr. The cars weren't the only noise he could hear. There was shouting and laughter—the sort of noises Scarlett and Jackson made. He wasn't sure it was them, but it was worth looking. The sounds were coming from very close by. If he was brave enough to go out onto the pavement, close to those cars, he was sure he could find the place.

Bootle dashed out, scurrying along low to the ground and pressing as far into the hedge as he could go. Every time a car went past—which wasn't very often, thankfully—he buried himself under the prickly, twiggy pieces at the bottom of the hedge and peered out, his blue eyes round and fearful.

The school was only a couple of hundred yards along the main road through the village, and on the same side as the lane. Bootle squirmed under the metal fence at the side of the playground and scuttled behind a wooden bench, where he sat, curled up as small as he could, and watched the children racing around the playground.

It was very noisy. He had thought Scarlett and Jackson were loud, but there were so many children here. And they were all wearing the same red sweaters and gray skirts, or shorts. He couldn't see Scarlett at all.

He shrank back behind the bench as a loud bell shrilled, and the children streamed back into the building on the far side of the playground. Then his ears pricked up, and he darted forward. That was Scarlett! Racing past him, with another girl. He mewed hopefully at her, but she'd already disappeared inside the white building.

The door was still open.

Bootle padded out into the empty playground and hurried over to the door. The noise of the children still echoed around the corridor, and he shivered a little. But if he wanted to find Scarlett, this was where he needed to be. He pattered along the chilly concrete floor, peeping in at the doors when he found an open one. The first classroom he looked into was full of children who were smaller than Scarlett, he thought. A little boy stared at him and pointed, his eyes widening delightedly. Bootle whisked out of the door as fast as he could. He had a feeling that he wasn't supposed to be here, and he didn't want to be caught before he'd found Scarlett.

The next couple of doors were shut, but then he found one ajar and looked around it. These children were more the right size. He sidled around the door, and then he saw her, facing away from him, but at the nearest table. The children were all looking away from the door, toward something at the other end of the classroom, so it was easy for Bootle to race across the carpet and hide under the table—right next to Scarlett's feet. He purred quietly to himself. He had done it! He'd found her!

Very gently, he rubbed the side of his head against Scarlett's sock.

Scarlett gave a tiny squeak, and Izzy stared at her. "What's the matter?"

"Something under the table..." Scarlett whispered, her eyes horrified. It was furry. What if it was one of those enormous furry spiders? There were definitely more spiders in the country. She'd found a huge one in the bathroom. Very slowly, she peered under the table, and Izzy looked, too.

"A cat!"

"Bootle!"

Mrs. Mason looked around sharply, and Izzy and Scarlett tried to look at the board and pretend there wasn't anything under their table.

Bootle purred louder and patted at

Scarlett's leg with a velvety paw.

"What's he doing here?" Izzy whispered as soon as Mrs. Mason had turned back to the board.

"He must have followed us again." Scarlett was grinning. She couldn't help it. She wasn't quite sure how she was going to work this out, but she loved it that Bootle wanted to be with her so much that he followed her all the way to school.

Bootle scrambled up onto her lap and sat there, purring and nudging at her school sweater.

Sarah and Millie saw a small orange head sticking up over the edge of the table and gasped. Scarlett put a finger to her lips and stared at them beseechingly. "Don't tell!" she whispered.

Sarah and Millie shook their heads, to say of course they wouldn't. But Mrs. Mason had seen them anyway.

"Scarlett, what's going on?" She came over to their table. "Oh, it's a kitten. What's he doing here?"

"He followed me from home," said Scarlett. "I'm sorry, Mrs. Mason. He was under the table—I didn't even know he was here till a minute ago."

She sighed a very tiny sigh. She'd hoped to keep Bootle a secret for a bit longer.

Mrs. Mason smiled. "Well, he's very sweet, but I'm afraid he can't stay in the classroom. You'd better take him up to the office and get Mrs. Lucy to call home. Is there someone there who can come and get him?"

Scarlett nodded. "My dad." She stood up, with Bootle snuggled against her, and the rest of the class whispered and aahed admiringly, reaching out to stroke him as she went out of the classroom.

"You're such a star for finding me!" Scarlett whispered, and Bootle purred.

Chapter Six

"I can't believe you followed me all the way, Bootle!" Scarlett told him again as she cuddled him in between putting her shoes on for school the next day. "Everybody wanted to know about you. Even people in the year above came to ask who you were—they saw me carrying you up to the office on their way back from PE." She sighed and placed him down on the stairs so she could put on her other shoe. "But Miss Wilson made Dad promise he wouldn't let it happen again. He said Miss Wilson was really scary. You're going to hate being shut up for the whole day." She petted his head, looking at him worriedly. "I guess in a few days you'll stop wanting to follow me. But I sort of wish you wouldn't. I love it that you're so smart!"

Bootle clambered up a couple of steps—it took a little while, because his legs were still very short—so that he could rub his chin on Scarlett's hair while she tied her shoe. He wasn't sure what she was saying, but it was definitely nice. She was fussing over him, and he liked to be fussed over.

Jackson came stomping down the hallway, and Scarlett turned around and dropped a kiss on the top of Bootle's little furry head. "I've got to go. Be good, Bootle!"

Bootle sat on the steps and stared at her sadly as she slipped quickly out of the front door, pulling it closed behind her. She had done it again! How many times did he have to follow them before she decided it would just be easier to take him with them? He jumped down the stairs in two huge leaps and made for the cat flap at a run. But it was locked. He scrabbled at it furiously, until Dad came and picked him up.

"Sorry, Bootle. Not happening, little one."

Bootle wriggled out of his arms and stalked away across the kitchen. He was going to follow Scarlett— somehow.

He would have to get out of the house a different way. Bootle prowled thoughtfully through the different rooms, sniffing hopefully at the front door to see if it might open. He could smell outside, but the door was very firmly shut. And so were all the windows.

But when Scarlett had taken him upstairs to play the day before, her window had been open. Bootle sat at the bottom of the stairs and gazed upward doubtfully. They were very big. But he could do it, if he was careful and slow.

Determinedly, he began to scrabble and haul himself up, stopping every so often for a rest, until at last he heaved himself onto the landing. His legs felt wobbly, but he made himself keep going, on into Scarlett's room, where the door was open just a crack. As soon as he pushed his way around the door, his ears pricked forward excitedly. The window was open! Just as he had remembered it!

Forgetting how tired his legs were, Bootle sprang up onto the bed, sniffing delightedly at the fresh air blowing in.

The windowsill was too far above the

bed for him to reach, though. His whiskers drooped a little. How was he going to get up there? He padded up and down the bed and stared at Scarlett's pile of cuddly toys. She liked to tease him with them, walking them up and down the bed for him to pounce on. But why shouldn't he climb up them instead? He put out a cautious paw, testing the back of a fluffy toy cat. It squashed down a little, but it was still a step up, and then onto the head of a huge teddy bear, and the stuffed leopard... and the windowsill!

Bootle pulled himself up, panting happily as he felt the cool breeze on his whiskers.

Now he only had to get down again on the outside…

"No kitten today?" Sarah asked Scarlett a little sadly.

Scarlett shook her head. "Miss Wilson made my dad promise he'd keep him in. Poor Bootle. He's going to be so sad."

"He's the smartest cat I've ever seen," Sarah told her admiringly. "Imagine coming all that way! And he'd never even been to the school before—I don't know how he figured out where to go!"

Scarlett smiled. "It's amazing, isn't it? I think he must have heard us all on the playground."

"You ought to stop in at the store and buy him a treat on the way home," Izzy suggested. "I've got some money, if you don't have any with you."

Scarlett nodded. "It's OK, I've got some. That's a really good idea." She grinned at Izzy. "You can help me choose." It was so nice having a friend come over—it felt like being back at her old school. Izzy's mom had been fine about her walking back with Scarlett—Izzy usually walked home, too. She had a big sister in Jackson's class.

"He might just about talk to us, if we bring him cat treats…"

Bootle scrabbled frantically at the branches of the creeper. It had looked so solid and easy to climb. But it turned out to be much harder to get down than up. It was also more wobbly, and he didn't like that. The first part had been easy, just a little jump to that sloping roof, then across the tiles. It was the drop down from the roof that was the problem. His claws were slipping. Bootle gave up trying to cling on and leaped out, as far away from the wall as he could, hoping that he remembered how to land.

He hit the ground with a jolt, but he was there! In the front yard, right by the gate and the lane. Bootle darted a glance behind him. Then he scrambled under the gate and set off to find Scarlett, trotting along jauntily. He knew the way now; he didn't have to sniff and search and worry.

He was halfway down the field when it started to rain. A very large drop hit him on the nose, making him shrink back. It was shortly followed by a lot of others, and in seconds his fur was plastered flat over his thin ribs. He hid in the hedge, his ears laid back.

He would wait for it to stop, Bootle decided, gazing out disgustedly. He certainly didn't want to go anywhere in that. But it went on and on, and he needed to find Scarlett. He put his nose out cautiously and shivered as he felt the drops on his whiskers. It was horrible.

But he couldn't stay here all day…

At last he slunk out from under the hedge, plodding through the wet muddy ruts and hoping that Scarlett would have something warm and dry to rub him with when he got to the school. He scurried down the pavement, through the puddles, so miserable that he didn't even bother to dart into the hedge to avoid the car going past. The driver of the car didn't see the soaked little kitten, and even if he had, he probably wouldn't have been able to avoid the huge puddle that splashed up over Bootle like a wave. There was so much water that he staggered back, letting out a mew of cold and dismay. Then he flat out ran for the school, racing across the playground toward that lovely, warm, open door.

But it was closed.

It had been wet, and no one had wanted the rain blowing in. All the doors were closed, every single one—as the soaked orange kitten found when he ran frantically all the way around the building.

Remembering the window he had climbed out of at home, Bootle looked up to see if there were any he could get through. There was a bench up against the wall, with a window right above it, and he jumped for the seat, scrabbling desperately until he could heave himself up. Then it was a little hop onto the arm, and then again onto the windowsill. But the window was shut, and everyone was gathered together at the other end of the classroom, looking at something and talking excitedly. They didn't hear him scratching hopefully at the window, and at last he jumped down.

Bootle sat under the bench and mewed miserably, calling for someone to come and let him in. He didn't care if they took him back to the cottage again, as long as he was out of the rain. He would stay at home and never try to follow anyone, if only he was dry.

No one came. No one heard him over the hammering and splashing of the rain, and the bench was dripping all over him. Bootle crawled out, looking around for another place to shelter. There were trees over on the edge of the path to the field. Maybe it would be drier there. He ran through the wet grass, shivering as the stems rubbed along his soaked fur and shaking water drops off his whiskers. He was so cold. Sitting still under the bench had made him shiver, and now he couldn't stop.

Then something made his ears flick up a little. There was another building. Just a little one, a shed, and he could see that the door was open!

Bootle made one last effort, forcing his shaky paws to race to the shed and struggle over the step and into the dusty dryness. He was so relieved to be out of the rain that he hardly noticed the sports equipment piled up all over the place—just the heap of old, tattered mats that he could curl up on for a rest.

It was while Bootle was fast asleep that the caretaker remembered he hadn't locked up the shed when he'd gotten out the spare chairs, and came grumpily back through the rain with his keys.

Chapter Seven

"Bootle!" Scarlett called happily as she opened the front door to let herself and Izzy and Jackson inside. "Bootle, come and see Izzy!"

Dad hurried out of the kitchen, a worried expression on his face. "You didn't see him in the lane?"

Scarlett stared at him. "What?" she asked with a frown.

"Bootle! He's not out there? I wondered if he'd slipped out somehow. He must have—I can't find him anywhere." Dad glanced distractedly up and down the hallway, as though he thought Bootle might pop out from behind the boots.

"You can't find him?" Scarlett stammered. "You mean—he's lost?"

"I'm sorry, Scarlett." Dad ran his fingers through his hair till it stood up on end. "I had a long phone meeting today, it finished about an hour ago. Then I went to find Bootle and check that he was all right, but he'd disappeared. I just don't understand how he got out!"

"Maybe he didn't," Izzy suggested shyly. "He could be stuck somewhere.

Olly's always doing that. He climbed into a drawer once and went to sleep, and my mom didn't see him and she shut the drawer. Then she got a real shock because her dresser was meowing."

"Maybe…" Dad murmured. But he looked doubtful. "Let's check again."

Scarlett grabbed Izzy's hand and pulled her up the stairs, while Jackson hurried into the living room.

"Bathroom," Scarlett muttered. "Not in here. The storage space, maybe?" She pulled the door open, but no indignant kitten darted out. "Jackson's room…" She peered in and called, "Bootle! Bootle! He isn't here, Izzy. I'm sure he'd come if he heard me calling. Or he'd meow to tell me where he was."

"He could be asleep. Try the other rooms, just in case."

Scarlett peered into her mom and dad's room, opening the closet, and all the drawers, but there weren't even any orange hairs. "This is my room," she told Izzy, pushing the last door open. "Bootle!" Scarlett caught her breath. She'd been hoping to find him asleep on her bed, but he wasn't there.

"Your window's open..." Izzy said slowly.

"Oh, but he couldn't get out through that." Scarlett shook her head. "It's really high."

Izzy frowned. "It depends how much he wanted to."

The girls climbed onto the bed so they could look out the window.

"You see? He could jump on there." Izzy pointed out the low part of the roof. "And there's all that ivy. That's like a cat ladder."

Scarlett stared at her. "You think he really could have climbed down that?"

Izzy looked down at the grass, which was an awfully long way away. "He might have."

Dad came in with Jackson behind. "He isn't in the house," he said grimly. "Was that window open, Scarlett?"

"Yes!" Scarlett nodded, her eyes filling with tears. "I'm really sorry, Dad. I didn't think Bootle would try to climb out of it! He can hardly get up the stairs, and the windowsill's really high."

"It isn't your fault." Dad put an arm around her. "I should have checked on him earlier. None of us realized he would be able to climb out of the window." He leaned over to look out. "I think he did, though. Some of that creeper's been torn away."

"Can we go and look for him?" Scarlett asked. "He might have tried to get to school again and got lost... Oh, Dad, what if he's gone on the road?"

Dad hugged her tighter. "Don't panic, Scarlett. I don't think he would, he's scared of the car noises. Remember how he meowed when we got him out of the car at the vet's? Even though he was safe in his basket he didn't like it when the cars went past. And why would he get mixed up about the way to school when he made it yesterday?" He let go of Scarlett and made for the door. "I'm just going to call the school and see if he's turned up there."

Scarlett sank down on her bed, staring up at Izzy. "I can't believe it. Everyone's been telling me today how lucky I am, and how gorgeous Bootle is, and now he's gone. I've only had him a couple of weeks, Izzy! How could I have lost him?"

It was starting to get dark. Bootle scratched at the door with his claws again, but they were starting to hurt. He'd hoped that he could make that little thin strip of light and fresh air bigger, maybe even big enough to squeeze out. But all he'd managed to do was scratch off some of the paint. Miserably, he sank down, mewing faintly. No one seemed to hear him, and it had been quite a while since he'd last heard anyone outside.

Maybe he would have to stay here all night, he thought anxiously. Scarlett wouldn't know where he was. Maybe she was looking for him? He stood up again quickly, even though his paws felt sore, and meowed as loud as he could. Scarlett would look for him, he was sure of it.

But even though he called and called and called to her, she didn't come, and at last he had to give up. He was worn out with scratching and meowing, and he dragged his sore paws back to the pile of mats. Then he curled up into a tight little ball and lay there in the gathering darkness, wondering how long it would be before anyone found him.

"We can make some LOST posters," Izzy suggested the next morning. "If we ask Mrs. Mason nicely, I bet she'll let us use the computer room. We could put them up all around the village on the way home."

Scarlett nodded. She should have thought of that the night before. After Izzy had gone home, she and Jackson had searched the house all over again, and then Scarlett had gone to bed and cried herself to sleep, knowing that her little kitten wasn't curled up in his basket in the kitchen—he was out there in the dark, and she had no idea where.

"We could go around to the houses between here and school and ask if anyone's seen him," she suggested, shivering at the thought of poor Bootle wandering around lost somewhere.

"Ooh, yes," Izzy agreed. "We could get people to check their garages. Don't worry, Scarlett, I can help with that. I know almost everybody in the village, and it's scary if you don't know people."

"That would be great," Scarlett said. She'd do anything if it meant finding Bootle, even if she had to talk to hundreds of grumpy people.

A couple older girls came past Scarlett and Izzy on their way in. "Hey, Scarlett! Did you get into trouble with Miss Wilson yesterday?" one of them asked.

Scarlett stared at her in bewilderment. "W-what?" she murmured, suddenly shy.

"When your kitten came back! I thought your brother said Miss Wilson had told your dad off. That he had to keep your kitten at home."

Scarlett forgot all about being shy. "You mean you saw Bootle? Are you sure it was yesterday?" she asked the older girl eagerly.

"Yeah, definitely..." The older girl— Scarlett was pretty sure she was called Eleanor—frowned. "I saw him looking in the classroom window, but then he ran off. Why? What's the matter?"

"Bootle's lost," Scarlett explained. "Dad had him shut in, but he climbed out of an upstairs window. We think he must have tried to follow us. We weren't sure he had made it to school, but if you saw him, then he was definitely here!"

"You're not mixing up the days?" Izzy asked Eleanor doubtfully.

Eleanor shook her head. "Nope. I'm certain. It was yesterday, when it was raining. And your kitten was soaked, Scarlett. His fur was actually dripping. I saw him out the window; he was on the playground. Before break, I think."

"He must have gotten out of the window really soon after we left," Scarlett murmured. "Thank you, Eleanor! I have to go and look for him!"

Chapter Eight

There was sunlight coming in from somewhere else, Bootle noticed, as the shed grew slowly lighter that morning. It wasn't just the space around the door. Where there was light, maybe there was some sort of hole, or another window that might be open, so he could climb through it.

It was up at the top, near the ceiling,

he thought. Very high up. Much higher than Scarlett's window. But then, there were a lot more things to climb in here. Piles of chairs, some benches, and more of those mats. He'd just have to find a way to reach it.

Bootle was sure that Scarlett was looking for him—almost sure, anyway. But the shed was all the way across the field from the school, he'd realized as he lay curled up on the mats. What if Scarlett didn't know about it? He couldn't wait for someone to let him out. He would have to do it for himself.

He stretched out his paws, which felt a little better this morning, though they still ached from all that scrabbling and scratching. Then he padded across the pile of mats and made a wobbly jump onto an old wooden bench. That was the first step…

"Where do we start?" Izzy asked as they hurried across the playground.

"I don't know. Maybe we should find Jackson and tell him that those girls saw Bootle," Scarlett suggested, but she couldn't see her brother anywhere, and she wanted to get started searching. "My dad called yesterday, remember? And he spoke to Mrs. Lucy in the office, and she went and asked in the staff room. No one had seen Bootle. So he wasn't just hanging around school looking for us."

Izzy frowned. "I know I keep going

on about him being shut in somewhere, but…"

Scarlett shook her head. "No, I think you're right! It's the only thing that makes sense. But where?"

Izzy shook her head. "I don't know. Maybe the classroom closets? Do you think if we asked Mrs. Lucy we could go and look? Oh no! There's the bell."

Scarlett looked anxiously around as everyone began to collect their stuff and head into school. "I can't go into school now! I can't! Bootle's here somewhere, I know he is!"

Izzy patted her shoulder. "It's OK. Look, we'll tell Mrs. Mason that Bootle might be here. We have to go in, Scarlett. We'll get in trouble otherwise."

Scarlett almost didn't care, but she supposed Izzy was right. Maybe they could ask the principal what to do. She'd said her dog used to follow her to school. She'd understand.

But Miss Wilson was talking to one of the teachers, and she just waved the girls past when Scarlett tried to hover in the doorway and talk to her.

Mrs. Mason was late coming into their class, and when she finally arrived she had her arms full of different colored PE jerseys, and she didn't look as though she wanted to hear about kittens, even though Izzy tried her best.

"Oh dear... Well, I'm sure you can take a look at break," she said distractedly when the girls tried to explain. "Sit down, please, you two."

Sit down! Scarlett opened her mouth to argue, but Mrs. Mason wasn't even looking at her anymore.

"Once we've done attendance, everyone, I've got some exciting news—we're going to start practicing for Sports Day. We've scheduled in a couple of extra PE sessions, and the first one is this morning. So let's just mark everyone in..." She moved names around on the whiteboard. "Where's Keisha? Is she still sick? OK."

"I don't want to do PE," Scarlett whispered frantically. "I have to go and look for Bootle!"

"PE!" Izzy nudged her. "I've just realized! Shut up in a shed, Scarlett, we said he could be!"

"What are you talking about?" Scarlett was biting back tears.

"There's a little shed at the end of the field, where Mr. Larkin, the caretaker, keeps stuff that doesn't get used all that much. He was definitely carrying chairs in and out yesterday; I heard him complaining about how wet he'd gotten."

"So the shed was open?" Scarlett breathed, her eyes widening.

Izzy nodded. "It must have been."

"Now go and get changed, please, everyone," Mrs. Mason called. "Then we'll go up to the hall, since it's still a little too wet on the field."

"I'm not getting changed," Scarlett

said, glaring at Izzy as though she thought her friend might tell her off. "I'm going to find Bootle."

Izzy shrugged. "Uh-huh, and I'm coming with you. Come on."

They hurried out of the classroom, ahead of everyone else, and Izzy grabbed Scarlett's hand. "It's this way. There's a side door. Come on." She pulled Scarlett down the corridor and pushed open a door Scarlett hadn't even known about. "Quick way out to the field."

"Hey, Izzy!" someone called. "We're in the hall, not the field! And you aren't changed!"

But Izzy and Scarlett were already running across the damp grass.

Bootle wobbled on the old chair. He was almost there—he could see the narrow wooden windowsill and the dirty pane of glass. The wind was shaking it as though it was loose. If he could only get to it, maybe he could push his way out, somehow.

He balanced himself again, teetering on the edge of the chair. He'd scrambled his way up the whole pile, and it had taken so long. If he misjudged his jump to the window, he wasn't sure he'd have the strength to climb up all over again. He was so hungry, and tired, and his paws hurt.

His whiskers flicked and shook as he tried to figure out how he could make the jump. It was much farther than he'd ever jumped before. And the strip of wood along the window was so small. But if it meant he could get out… Then he would go back home and wait there for Scarlett. He would see if he could get back in through the cat flap.

He tensed his muscles to spring and crouched there, trembling a little, trying to summon up the courage to leap.

Then his ears twitched. He could hear something! People talking!

"Bootle! Bootle, are you in there? Is the door locked, Izzy?"

That was Scarlett!

Bootle let out a shrill desperate meow and forgot to worry about how narrow the ledge was. He just went for it, scrabbling madly with his paws as he almost made it, and then heaving himself up onto the windowsill.

Then he batted his paws against the glass, mewing frantically.

"I can hear him! He *is* in there, Izzy, you were right!"

"It's locked. I'll go and get Mr. Larkin."

Bootle heard feet thudding away and cried out in panic. They hadn't heard him! They were going!

"It's OK, Bootle. Where are you?"

There were noises outside and Bootle banged his nose against the grubby window, trying to see what was happening.

Scarlett pulled herself up onto the little tiny ledge on the outside of the window. "I can see you! It's really you, Bootle. Oh, I've been so worried. I can't believe you climbed out of a window." She giggled with relief, and sniffed. "And now you're trying to climb out of this one, aren't you, silly kitten."

Bootle mewed and scraped, but the window wouldn't open. How was he going to get to Scarlett?

"Oh! Mr. Larkin! The keys!" Scarlett's face disappeared from the window, and Bootle wriggled himself around as the door rattled and shook. And then it opened.

With a joyful yowl, he bounded back to the wobbly chair and took a flying leap to the mats, and then Scarlett was there, hugging him.

Bootle purred and purred, and rubbed his face against hers, and purred louder.

"Izzy! Scarlett! What are you doing out here? Oh! Oh, no, has he been shut in here?" Mrs. Mason peered worriedly into the dusty shed.

"All night," Scarlett told her, shivering. "Can I call my dad, Mrs. Mason, please? Can I take him home?"

Mrs. Mason nodded. "Yes, you'd better take him up to the office again. I hope he doesn't keep doing this, Scarlett."

Scarlett stroked Bootle, who was pressed against her sweater like he never meant to let go. "Me, too."

"Well, he got soaking wet and trapped in a shed, so maybe he'll stay at home now," Izzy suggested.

Scarlett nodded. "He looks like he wants to go home," she agreed, feeling the sharp little points of Bootle's claws hooked into her sweater. "I promise I won't ever let you get lost again," she whispered to him, feeling his whiskers brush across her cheek. "I'll look after you always."

"I'm really glad my mom said I could come back with you." Izzy sighed happily, and blew on her hot chocolate.

Scarlett nodded, stroking Bootle, who was curled up on her lap with his claws hooked determinedly into her school skirt. He wasn't letting her go. "We might never have figured out where he was if it wasn't for you! He could have been stuck in there forever—until Mr. Larkin had to put the chairs away again."

Bootle purred as Scarlett gently rubbed behind his ears. He was finally starting to feel nice and warm again. Scarlett's dad had lit the fire in the living room, and the girls were huddled in front of it—it was raining again, so it had been a wet walk home. They'd splashed through the puddles as fast as they could, anxious to see Bootle again and check that he was OK.

"Do you want any more hot chocolate, girls?" Dad asked. "Jackson's having another cup."

Scarlett shook her head. "No, thanks."

Izzy smiled at him. "No, that's OK, thanks. It was delicious. It's a pity cats can't have hot drinks, though. Bootle must have been frozen after a night in the shed."

"I've had him on my lap ever since I picked him up," Dad told them. "Apart from when he was wolfing down a huge dinner and breakfast in one. He definitely wanted company, and since he couldn't have you, Scarlett, I was the next best thing."

"I hope he's not going to follow us again tomorrow," Scarlett said, looking down at him anxiously. He didn't look very adventurous at the moment…

Dad shook his head. "No, I'm sure he'll remember being trapped. He won't want that to happen again. But I promise I will make sure every window's closed. I'll even let him play with the computer, Scarlett." He grinned. "I'll find him one of those homework websites—then he won't need to go to school."

Bootle stretched out his paws and stared up at them in surprise as they laughed, and then he huddled himself back into the front of Scarlett's sweater. It was lovely and warm inside. And dry. He hadn't realized how damp and miserable it could be, following people. For the moment, he was going to stay right here.